MADDIE
Visits the Pharmacist

Story by Donna Keissami

Illustrated by Kresnha Zulkarnaen

Published by Donna Keissami, Irvine, California

Text copyright © Donna Keissami, 2014
Illustrations copyright © Kresnha Zulkarnaen, 2014
Edited by Marya Jansen-Gruber
Layout and Design by Donna Keissami

ISBN-13: 978-1493768165
ISBN-10: 1493768166
LCCN: 2013922356
Printed in the United States of America
10 9 8 7 6 5 4 3 2 1
First Edition

This book is dedicated to my husband, Arash, who supported me throughout the book creation process, and who helped me make my dream of writing a children's storybook come true. This book is also dedicated to my son, Dean, whose existence pushed me to complete this book. You have both immensely enriched my life and my love for you is eternal.

Maddie turns seven next week. She can't wait to grow up! This year is particularly special. Her mom told her that she can throw a dragon-themed birthday party. Dragons are Maddie's favorite! She is so excited that she starts to count down the days.

PARTY

On Friday after school, Maddie and her mother go to the party store, and they buy dragon balloons, dragon invitations, dragon party treats, a "pin-the-tail-on-the-dragon" game, and dragon plates and cups. Maddie can't wait to have her party!

On Monday, five days before Maddie's birthday party, Maddie is sitting in class at school when she starts to feel sick.

Her throat is sore, she feels hot all over, she is tired, and her stomach hurts. The nurse takes one look at Maddie, and she decides to call the little girl's mother.

Maddie's mother takes Maddie straight to Dr. Daisy's office.

"Stick your tongue out Maddie, and say 'Ahhhhh' for me please," Dr. Daisy says. Maddie feels too miserable to argue, so she sticks out her tongue.

"I am going to touch the back of your throat with this soft swab, Maddie. I know it will feel funny, but it won't hurt. I promise."

The swab does make Maddie's throat tickle, but that is all. Maddie is glad to close her mouth and snuggle up against her mother while Dr. Daisy runs a test.

"It looks as though you have strep throat, Maddie. This is not a serious illness, and if you rest and take the medicine I am going to order for you, you should feel a lot better in a day or two."

On their way home, Maddie's mom picks up Maddie's antibiotic medicine from the pharmacy. While they wait for the medicine, Maddie sits with her mother, holding her favorite dragon close. She can't wait to go home.

"Maddie, honey, you need to take your medicine now," Maddie's mom says as soon as they get home, and she starts to pour the medicine onto a medicine spoon. "I am not going to take that stuff," says Maddie. She frowns at the medicine bottle, and pouts at her mother.

"Honey, if you don't take your medicine, you won't get better, and we won't be able to have your birthday party on Saturday."

"I won't take that medicine!" Maddie says, stamping her foot. A large lump fills her sore throat, her eyes start to fill, and though she tries hard not to cry, tears start to spill down her cheeks, landing on the head of her favorite dragon.

No matter what Maddie's mother says, Maddie refuses to take her medicine. She sits on her bed and cuddles her dragon. At least *he* isn't trying to make her take nasty tasting medicine!

Maddie's mother makes a telephone call, and then she and Maddie go back to the pharmacy.

"I hear that you are having trouble taking your medicine, Maddie," says the pharmacist.

"I don't like medicine," Maddie says.

"I understand, Maddie, but if you don't take it, you are going to get sicker and sicker. Don't you want to help your poor body get better?"

"Yes I do," Maddie mumbles into her dragon's soft fur. The nasty lump in her throat comes back, and she angrily squeezes her eyes tight to keep the tears from coming.

PHARMACY

"Why don't you like medicine, Maddie?" the pharmacist asks. She smiles at the little girl. "It always tastes so horrible, and it makes me feel even sicker," Maddie explains. "Do you like grape-flavored candy, Maddie?" the pharmacist asks.

"Oh yes!" Maddie says, thinking about the grape lollipop that she had a few days ago. "When your mother brought me your prescription earlier, I added grape flavor to your medicine so that it wouldn't taste bad. Did you know that?"

"No!" Maddie is surprised to learn that medicine can have a nice taste added to it. "I tried to tell her about what you did, but she wasn't really interested in listening to me at the time," Maddie's mother says, giving Maddie a wink.

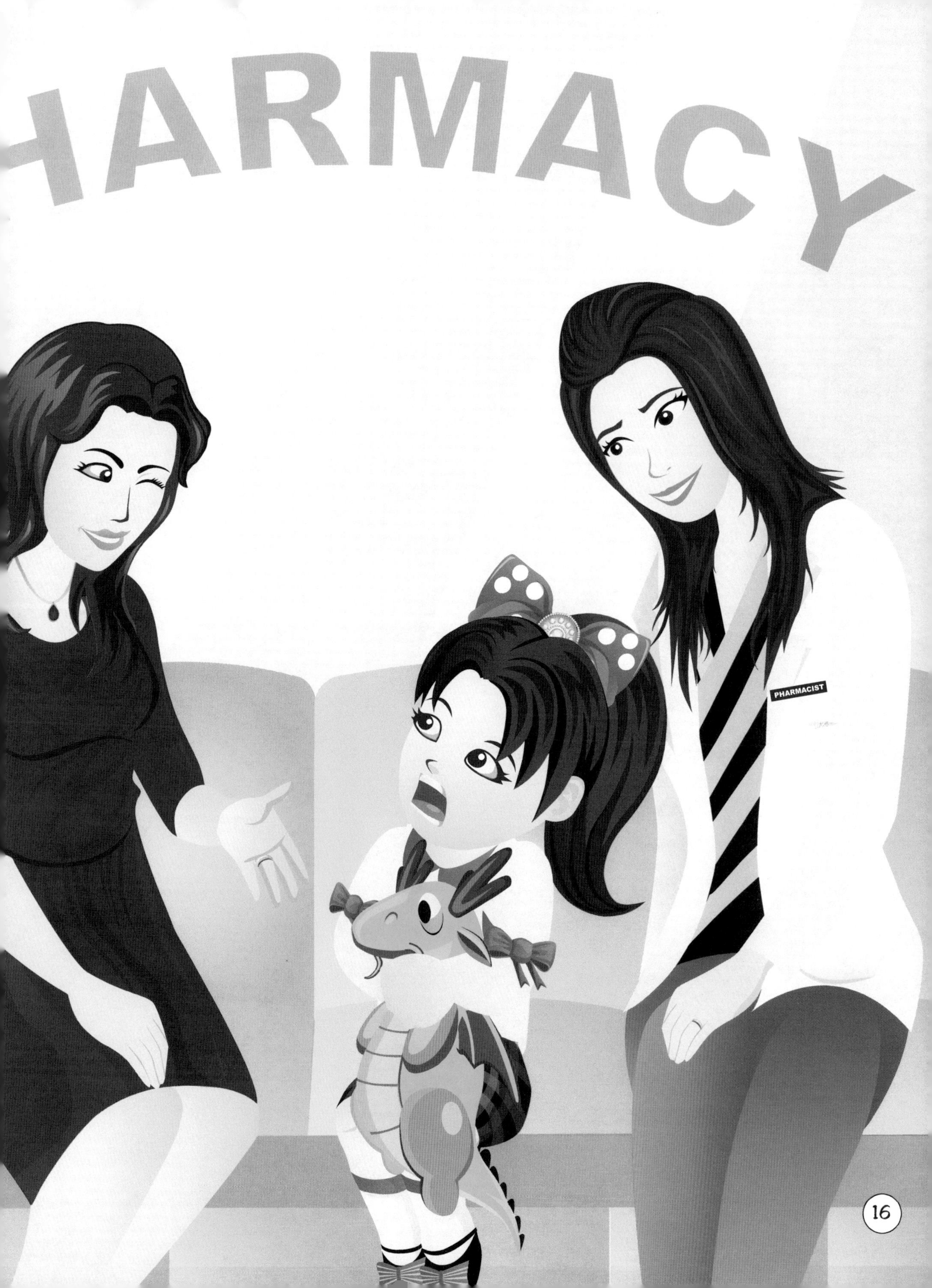
HARMACY
PHARMACIST

The pharmacist shows Maddie all the bottles of flavoring that she uses to make children's medicines taste nice. She even lets Maddie smell the liquid inside a few of the bottles. Mmmmm, the cherry one smells quite good.

"I have one little boy who always chooses the cherry flavor for his medicine," the pharmacist tells Maddie. "Oh, and I have a dog who really likes the banana flavoring."

"A dog?" Maddie laughs.

"Yes. I prepare prescriptions for pets too, and I have special flavors for them, like chicken and fish. This dog doesn't like the chicken flavor; he likes the banana one."

Then the pharmacist lets Maddie choose a medicine spoon for herself. Maddie chooses a green one because it matches the color of her dragon's fur. "You can help your mom give you the medicine by filling up the spoon for her," the pharmacist says. "Can we try it right now?" Maddie asks. "Of course Maddie," smiles her mother.

Maddie carefully fills her special green medicine spoon with her grape-flavored medicine. Her mother then checks to make sure that there is the right amount of medicine in the spoon. Then her mother puts the spoon in Maddie's mouth. "Mmmmm," says Maddie. The medicine tastes a lot like the grape lollipop that she had.

Before Maddie leaves the pharmacy, the pharmacist gives her a coloring book, and she reminds Maddie to make sure that she takes all the medicine in the bottle.

"Even when you start to feel better, you have to keep taking your medicine, or the strep will come back. Okay, Maddie?" "Okay," Maddie says, and she gives the pharmacist a hug.

At home, Maddie rests in bed, and she colors in her new coloring book using all kinds of bright colors. She takes her medicine without making a fuss. After a few days at home, Maddie starts to feel a lot better, and she is able to go back to school.

On Saturday, Maddie has her dragon party. The house is all decorated, Maddie's mom has made a fantastic dragon-shaped cake, and there is a special guest at the party.

Maddie invited the pharmacist to come to her birthday celebration, and the pharmacist has come.

She has brought Maddie a wonderful present, and it is...

...a lovely purple dragon who is wearing a little white pharmacist's coat!

49823024R00018

Made in the USA
Lexington, KY
21 February 2016